A Stable Birth

A Story About

the Birth of Jesus Christ

June G. Paul

Lovstad Publishing
Poynette, Wisconsin
www.Lovstadpublishing.com

A STABLE BIRTH
REVISED EDITION
(Previously published as *A Stable Birth*, ISBN 978-1-499008692)

The conversations in this story are fictional except
for quotations from *The Holy Bible*.
Scripture taken from *The Holy Bible*, New International
Version.® Copyright © 1973, 1978, 1984 Biblica. Used with
permission from Z o n d e r v a n.

ISBN: 0692312889
ISBN-13: 978-0692312889

Printed in the United States of America

Cover design by Lovstad Publishing
Cover photo by June Paul

Additional copies available for order at
www.junegpaul.net

This book is dedicated to the Glory of God
In Thanksgiving for the birth and eternal life of Jesus Christ

and

In honor of the men and women who bore witness to his birth.

For God so loved the world that he gave his one and only Son, that whoever believes in him shall not perish but have eternal life. For God did not send his Son into the world to condemn the world, but to save the world through him.

John 3:16-17

CONTENTS

My soul glorifies the Lord and my spirit

rejoices in God my Savior, for he has been

mindful of the humble state of his servant.

Mary ~ betrothed to Joseph, mother of Jesus.

Luke 1:46—48

ACKNOWLEDGMENTS

I would like to thank the members of Pauquette Wordcrafters and The Writers at the Portage for their constant encouragement to keep writing. My sister, Niki, is also a great encourager of mine.

Thank you to Caroline, Sue, and Sarah for helping me with editing and to Rev. Mike Tess for giving me encouragement and prayerful support in my life and my writing. Thank you, also, to Joel at Lovstad Publishing for all his help in making sure I had a book on time.

I would be remiss if I failed to thank my Sunday School teachers, clergy, and women in ministry positions. I also want to thank the professors at Edgewood College who helped me study the Scriptures, to think in deeper ways about their relevance in the lives of people in Biblical times and our own culture and generation.

Last, but not least, I want to thank Kate, my friend and editor, for all her help, encouragement, and enthusiasm over this book and future projects.

Blessings to everyone!

June G. Paul

October 2014

JUNE G. PAUL

A Stable Birth

JUNE G. PAUL

PREFACE

For Christians, Christmas is a time to celebrate the birth of Jesus Christ, the Prince of Peace, Messiah, Savior of the world. This celebration is more deeply appreciated when we recognize the fullness of God's favor, grace, and mindfulness towards humanity as we tell and hear about his birth. It is a reminder to us of God's faithfulness and love.

The title of this book reflects not only the circumstances of where Jesus was born, but also the stability of the faith residing in the lives of Mary, Joseph, and other characters in the story. When it came time to publish the story, I began second-guessing the title. I went back to God in prayer and became convinced the title should remain.

This story is part fact, part fiction. The characters are factual. I have intentionally not named minor characters so the readers will not be influenced by names. It is enough for us to know the names of the main characters in this story. Most of the conversations contained in this story are not recorded in Scripture; they are just what I think and imagine might have occurred at the time of Jesus' birth.

Woven within the story of the physical birth of Jesus, God Come to Earth, are the stories of people being reborn spiritually, stories of hope renewed in the belief of the promises contained in the Scriptures, and the fulfillment of God's love and care for all of creation. God's faithfulness to Mary and Joseph is clear.

In Biblical times, women were not highly esteemed. Seeing women such as Mary and Elizabeth lifted up is a sign of God's love and favor towards all people regardless of age, gender, nationality, or genealogical record.

While it is amazing to think about Mary's response to God's desire for her to give birth to the Savior, it is equally amazing to think about Joseph's courage in accepting God's desire for him: to take Mary for his wife. Though they experienced rejection and difficulties because they followed God's will, they experienced greater peace in God's favor towards them for their humble submission.

I hope you enjoy the book and are inspired to read the Bible and learn more about the child named Jesus who grew up to become known as The Prince of Peace. The New Testament chapters of The Holy Bible, regardless of the translation, record much of the life and teachings of Jesus. As you read this book, please take time to think and pray about your willingness to learn about and submit to God's plan to use you and your life to glorify him and benefit others.

A Stable Birth

THE EVENING OF HIS BIRTH

"Joseph, I... I think the time is near!" Mary breathed laboriously. "I... I... I can't go on any longer. We have to stop! I think our baby is ready to be born!" Mary was almost doubled over in pain, rubbing her abdomen with one hand while her other was pressed onto her forehead, head bowed down.

Maybe Joseph, holding the reins of their donkey and walking a little ahead of Mary while keeping an eye on her and the ground in front of them as they went from inn to inn looking for a room, maybe he turned to look closer at her, or maybe he looked up to the heavens, or both while he wondered, *Now?*

"Now?!" Joseph asked out loud. He wasn't sure if Mary had called out "Ow!" or "Now!" But he heard her clearly say, "We need to find a place now! I cannot wait! Our son is going to be delivered soon!"

Joseph had never heard Mary sound so stern or serious or in so much agony. He asked one innkeeper after another if they had a room available for the night. *No... no... no.* Frantically, he knocked hard on the door of yet another inn. The innkeeper looked through a window, shook his head no, and then pulled the curtain shut. This time, Joseph couldn't take no for an answer. Looking at Mary, he knocked harder on the door. The curtain on the window remained closed. He knocked again and called out, "Please!" The door opened, and the innkeeper stood with lantern in hand staring at Joseph.

"Please," Joseph begged looking toward Mary, then back at the innkeeper, "she is in labor." He spoke quietly to the innkeeper now, looking him in the eye. "If you have no room for us to stay, do you know another who does, or do you have a place where she can rest for a bit and deliver our child if she must?"

The innkeeper looked at Joseph, noting the depth of his urgent request, then looked toward Mary sitting on the donkey. Holding the child within her womb, she braced herself for the next contraction. He turned back toward Joseph with a more understanding expression on his bearded face. Looking again into the innkeeper's eyes, Joseph spoke in a near whisper, "Please, do you have a place where she might deliver our child? We're here to register for the census, but it's obvious the child is coming now."

Looking upon Joseph and Mary with compassion, the innkeeper nodded yes, retreated to get a second lantern, and came back outside to meet Mary in the still of the night. He smiled at her and spoke to the young couple, "You two can follow me. I do have a place to offer you, if you find it acceptable. It isn't much, but it might do for your need at this time."

Joseph placed his arm around Mary's waist and gently helped her down from the donkey's back. As her feet touched the ground, she gasped. Another contraction took hold and wrapped around her womb fiercely. She leaned heavily on Joseph's arm, squeezing his hand. The strength with which she held onto him surprised Joseph. Once the contraction loosened its grip on her, Mary loosened her grip on Joseph's hand. Joseph leaned toward her gently asking, "Are you able to walk now, Mary? Or shall I carry you?"

Looking up into his eyes Mary smiled, "I think I can walk now, Joseph; we can follow him and walk together."

Slowly and steadily, they followed the innkeeper over to and down the rough rock-hewn steps into his stable. He slid the heavy gate door open and looked at the couple. "This is all I have available if you want to stay the night and deliver your child here." Joseph looked in quickly then turned toward Mary. She was arching her back and pressing her hands against her spine as she nodded yes, all while letting out a deep, guttural sigh. She turned to the innkeeper and smiled demurely while looking downward. Joseph answered the innkeeper and nodded his head. "This will do then, thank you."

The innkeeper walked in ahead of Joseph and Mary, hung the second lantern on the hook hanging from the central rafter, and started walking out of the stable. Nearing the door, he glanced back. There was no midwife. Noticing the two of them trying to get comfortable, he wondered about their supplies, and before drawing the gate door of the stable closed, he spoke.

"I'll leave the door to the inn unlatched tonight. That way, if you need anything, you can come and wake me, even if it's before the cock crows. Make use of whatever supplies you need that you find here. There's a well around the corner; I'll bring you some water. You can heat it over the fire pit." He leaned his head toward the fire pit and asked, "Do you need anything else? Blankets? Food?"

Joseph walked toward the innkeeper, "You're very generous, thank you; the water and fire pit are sufficient. We have blankets and food enough for now. I don't believe we'll be eating tonight." He chuckled quietly but a little nervously as well. He was a carpenter by trade, neither as knowledgeable nor comfortable with the birthing process as a shepherd or farmer might be. The innkeeper was unaware of Joseph's trade at this time and assumed Joseph would ask for help if he needed it. Joseph was trusting in help from God and his betrothed.

Mary's faith amazed Joseph; she had displayed a tremendous amount of courage during her pregnancy. Mary was also impressed with Joseph's trust in God throughout the past months. Together they helped each other find encouragement from the angelic messengers and their instruction to have no fear. Daily, Mary and Joseph grew in faith and confidence of God's promises.

The innkeeper bowed his head as he bade them goodbye while drawing the gate door closed. Joseph walked toward the corner to start a fire in the pit. "How are you doing, Mary?" he asked once they were alone.

"I'm fine Joseph; just a little overwhelmed, that's all. Overwhelmed and a little tired yet wide awake somehow." She smiled at Joseph as he rose from the fire and walked toward her with the supplies that had been wrapped in a blanket. As he prepared the bedding and spread out the blanket for Mary to lie down, it struck him—God had chosen a child bride for Himself and commissioned Joseph to care for and protect her, protect them. He drew strength and peace from Mary's demonstration of courage in this remarkable journey and calling from the Lord God on her life, on their lives.

The innkeeper came back in quietly with a basin and pitcher full of warm water and, without a word, set it upon the fire pit. He left the stable unnoticed by both Mary and Joseph. While Joseph continued preparing the bedding for his betrothed, the soon-to-be mother of Jesus, he recalled the struggle he had when she came to him with the news that she was pregnant.

They were betrothed when she had come to tell him she was 'with child.' He had been angry, and she had been frightened by his reaction, yet she had remained adamant and courageous in defense of herself. *It's the Lord's doing, Joseph! Not mine! I haven't been with a man! You have to believe me, Joseph. I am your betrothed. I wouldn't be unfaithful toward you!*

Joseph had dropped his carpenter tools in disbelief and raised his voice. *How can that be, Mary? It's impossible!* He had raised his arms over his head, and she had jumped back away from him, almost cowering. She knew what happened to women who had been caught in adultery.

Joseph, please believe me. I'm telling you the truth! This is God's doing and will. I wouldn't lie to you Joseph! Oh Joseph... She had covered her face and fallen to the floor.

Joseph had walked around his workbench to where she was and looked at her. He bent over, put his hands on her arms, and lifted her up as she trembled. He loved her, but the laws were strict.

Mary! How can I take you for my wife? Certainly, I will be disgraced! Our family name will be ruined! How can God do this to you? To me? To us! Mary, you can't be with child without being with a man. Did someone force himself on you? Mary, tell me the truth!

He had looked squarely into her eyes, and hers had met his directly as she answered him, *I have told you the truth Joseph! The angel...* Before she could finish her sentence, Joseph had cut her off and sent Mary away. He had been so angry and distraught that morning. He hadn't believed a word she had told him until later that evening when he was alone, and the angel had visited him.

Now, they were together tonight, both trusting the messages from God's angelic messengers. Mary had been considered 'able' by God to bring his Son, Immanuel, into this world, into their family. The angel had told Joseph he should not be afraid to take Mary as his wife. Until then, Joseph had planned to divorce her. If he had, she might have been stoned to death. Joseph understood that God was entrusting him to care for Jesus and his mother on God's behalf. It seemed a huge burden and a mighty blessing all at the same time.

Joseph recalled all these events as he helped Mary down into the bedding. Now that she was lying down, he gently rubbed her back. He knelt at her side, whispered a prayer, and waited quietly. As Mary's labor progressed, he wiped her forehead, helped her to reposition, rubbed her back again, held her stomach, and felt her contractions. Instead of crying out in pain, Mary breathed in deeply and blew each breath out slowly and deliberately while coaching Joseph through the delivery. Joseph was the first person on earth to hold the Savior of the World in his hands.

The delivery happened so quickly that Joseph and Mary both forgot the long hours of labor as soon as they held Jesus. Both contemplated whom it was they had brought into the world: God's own son. Mary watched Joseph lift their child into his arms and wrap him in a cloth before he placed Jesus in her arms.

Leaning over the precious child and his mother, Joseph kissed the baby Jesus on his forehead. Then he glanced at Mary gazing into her son's eyes. She caressed Jesus' cheek and fingers, then drew him toward her face. Mary ran her forefinger down his small arm and over his hand. She touched Jesus' ear, kissed him on his tiny, perfectly formed lips, and then lifted him toward Joseph, asking him to bathe their Savior son.

Joseph held Jesus over the basin of clean water that he had reserved, and while pouring water over the Christ child said, "Your name is Jesus because you will save people from their sins." Then he wrapped Jesus in a blanket and brought him back to Mary. She was speechless. Mary's heart beat rapidly as she looked into his eyes. She was overcome with a reverent sense of awe as she held her Savior in her arms. A tear welled up from the depths of her soul, spilled out of her eye, and slid down her cheek, falling quietly on Jesus' forehead.

Mary leaned over and kissed Jesus on his hands and lips then pressed her cheek to his forehead and held him closely for a moment. When Mary moved him away from her cheek over to her shoulder, he stirred a little, crying ever so quietly, his breath clean and soft on her neck. Mary lowered Jesus to her breast and nursed him.

Joseph began cleaning the cloths that had been used during the delivery. When he finished rinsing them, he took the basin of water out of the stable, threw it on the ground, and shoveled some dirt over it. Then he returned to the stable to sit near Mary and Jesus. He marveled at this miracle birth and talked with Mary about who their child was.

"Mary, this is God's son; he has been born for everyone in the world. He is ours to hold for but a little while. We must hold him loosely so Jesus can become the Savior of the world as God has planned."

Joseph placed his arm around Mary and Jesus and rested his cheek on the top of Mary's head. Their hearts and minds were so full of wonder they could not speak anymore, only be still and know that Jesus was God's Son, born to save people from sin.

In that holy moment, as the moon rose and the stars lit up the night sky, it seemed the whole earth and everything in it was standing still. It was in this stillness that Mary, Joseph, and Jesus all fell asleep together on a bed of straw with blankets thrown over them. In the morning, the innkeeper would come with his wife to offer them warm food and beverage. For now, they had all they needed: the Love of God with them.

THE SHEPHERDS IN THE FIELDS

The night was calm and the air brisk as the shepherds in the near countryside decided to settle themselves around their flock. They were traveling alongside a caravan through the Judean region. They had herded and led their flock almost 12 miles today. After stopping to let them graze and water a few times, they felt quite proud of their accomplishment. They began counting the sheep again, to be sure they hadn't lost any and to make certain none were ill or had any injuries. Gathering around the base of a carob tree, the shepherds talked about their flock and wondered how far ahead the owner was and when he would let them know where they would be setting up their tents for the season.

"It appears we are fortunate today, no injuries!"

"A blessing indeed that we haven't lost any on this part of our journey. Not a one was injured or attacked!"

"Yes! And a blessing also, that we haven't had to stop for a single birth so far. Of course, it's not the season, but it seems there are always some born out of season."

"I wonder how much further we will have to travel before our master sets up the tent city. Perhaps he will send a servant back and tell us this is as good an area as any."

"That would be good with me! The sheep have plenty to graze upon, and the trees are mature and large enough to provide shelter from the storms and the sun. I don't know how far ahead the rest of the caravan is."

"Perhaps just over the hill on the other side of this grove of trees. But let's rest; we can look tomorrow. If we are too far behind, he will send one of his servants to find us."

They began gathering some dry wood that had fallen from older trees and dug a pit for a small fire so they could cook food and keep themselves warm. Sitting around the fire while eating their evening meal, they talked about who would take the first watch while the others slept.

In the wilderness, even on the edge of the city, it was important to watch for the wild animals that stalked the flock. Wolves were tenacious, hiding in caves during the day and coming out in the evenings to hunt their prey. They were swift, and the color of their dark coats blended well with the night sky and landscape, making it easy for them to capture more than one sheep at a time, especially the younger, weaker ones.

The previous year, their flock had been attacked, and they had lost over a dozen sheep. Their master was not pleased, but fortunately, he was kind-hearted and kept the shepherds in his employ. Another master might have terminated them or accused them of selling or trading the sheep and had them arrested. Some shepherds of low character did do those things. But the three shepherds who agreed to take the first watch had been with their master's family and each other since birth. Their fathers had raised them with integrity and had instilled good character traits into their work habits.

The tent city people also had herders with smaller

groups of goats and cattle. They were camping out on the other side of the stream, having traveled alongside the shepherds at about the same pace. They had arrived a little earlier because they had fewer animals to herd. Their fire was lit, and a couple shepherds were sleeping around it while the others walked among the animals. Movement of human beings had a tendency to ward off the creeping in of predators, both animal and human.

Yes, there were thieves who lived in the caves outside of town. The world has never been quite free of evil, for some have never been able to subdue themselves and their desires. Others have not been taught and so, as outlaws, become outcasts until thrown into prison. It was rare for shepherds to be able to catch the thieves single-handedly, so the owners learned that having multiple shepherds for their flocks was in their best interest.

Thus it was, the night Jesus was born, the fields were filled with shepherds tending their flocks as they had every other night of the year. The occasional sound of sheep stirring in their sleep mingled with the music of water trickling and spilling over the rocks in the streambed; the croaking of an occasional frog and the hoot of a night owl keeping predators at bay mixed with the far-off howl of wolves; all these sounds filtered through the air. The sky was a clear, midnight blue hue with a scattering of soft gray and white clouds.

Suddenly, a wind blew the clouds away, and the stars twinkled, so numerous it looked like a field full of fireflies. One of the shepherds glanced up to look at them when he noticed the sky begin to glow, but it was not from the moon or the stars. The glowing came from no specific light and began covering the sky, brighter than the moon, softer than the sun. He looked at the sheep and saw they were no longer shadowed with darkness. The other shepherds began looking upward, and those sleeping awoke. The owl and wolves ceased their songs, as did the frogs and crickets. In the stillness, a new sound, from far off, began filling the air. The cooing of a morning dove was heard ever so slightly, and suddenly there was a heavenly chorus singing.

The shepherds looked to each other for recognition, affirmation that what they saw and heard was real and not a dream. They trembled, shaking their heads, raising their shoulders and arms across their faces to shield their eyes from this brightness. Some turned in circles to look for the source of the light and chorus of voices. But the voices and light were clearly descending from above them, over a hill? No, there was no hill that high.

A form became visible, yet not distinguishable in bodily form, a shadow of the brightest light they had ever seen. As the shepherds dropped to their knees, an angelic voice rang out full and strong above the chorus. The message echoed through the field, filling their ears and minds and stirring them to the depth of their souls.

> "Do not be afraid! I bring you good news of great joy that will be for all the people. Today in the town of David a Savior has been born to you; he is Christ the Lord. This will be a sign to you: You will find a

baby wrapped in cloths and lying in a manger... Glory to God in the highest, and on earth peace to men on whom his favor rests.[1]

Some shepherds almost cowered under the announcement, yet they kept looking at one another. As the angels receded into the heavens, the shepherds composed themselves. They looked over their flocks, which had remained calm, sleeping as if nothing had happened. Rising, the shepherds went to their fire pits, spoke about what they had heard and seen, and agreed they would immediately go search for the sign in Bethlehem.

They ran together swiftly. Talking about the sign, one shepherd called out. "This must be the sign the prophet Isaiah spoke about! I did not expect to be alive to see this sign! This is an incredible experience! This was foretold to mankind years ago!"

Another shepherd encouraged the others to run faster so they could get back to watching their flocks. Another prayed to the Lord, "God have mercy on us and protect our sheep. Help us to find the sign, to find our Savior, Christ the Lord, and to return quickly and safely with no harm to anyone."

Oddly enough, the shepherd lagging behind was the first to see the place where the star seemed to be resting above. He ran quickly to catch up with the rest of the shepherds, calling out loudly, "There! See! A stable with the glory of the Lord shining on it! That must be the place where we will find the baby, lying in a manger. Be still, be quiet; we don't want to startle him."

The shepherds slowed down and went to look in the window. Joseph woke quickly and rose to his feet. The shepherds backed away from the window as Joseph came near.

"Who are you?" Joseph asked. "What are you looking for? Why are you here?" Thinking they were thieves, he was ready to defend his family and the innkeeper's property.

One shepherd answered while the others stood behind him nodding in agreement. "We are not enemies or thieves, we mean you no harm. We are shepherds in search of the sign of the Savior."

Mary was awake now. Joseph looked at her, and both were stunned by the words the shepherds had used. Joseph walked carefully toward them.

"And how do I know you mean no harm? What sign are you looking for?" Joseph kept questioning them as he walked to the gate door. "What are you doing out at this late hour of the night? Who told you about a sign of the Savior? Are you drunk and out of your minds?" Joseph was a little sarcastic with his questioning so as to discern the purity of their motives.

"No, please sir, we are not drunk. We are mere shepherds. We were tending our flocks when, well..." The shepherd who had begun speaking first seemed to be at a loss for words.

Another stepped forward and spoke, "Please, sir, I pray to God you will believe us. An angel of the Lord appeared to us from out of the heavens while we were watching our sheep tonight. We were shaken by the presence of this angel."

A third shepherd spoke, "Not only by the angel's

presence, but by the message he proclaimed with such authority and by the heavenly host that accompanied him."

They had walked along the side of the stable. Now they were talking outside the gate door, patient enough not to force Joseph to open it.

"And what was the message the angel proclaimed?" Joseph asked them. Remembering his own experience with the angel of the Lord and that of Mary, he looked at her and Jesus. *If they have received the same message,* he thought to himself, *I will let them see Jesus.*

The shepherds all began speaking at once, their voices mingling and words crossing over each other. But Joseph was able to hear clearly.

"The sky was filled with light, and the angel's voice broke through the stillness of the night saying we shouldn't be afraid. Not to be afraid, that he had good news, glad tidings. We would find a sign, and the sign would be that we would find a baby in the city of David. A baby wrapped in cloth and lying in a manger. And there was more: the angel said the babe is Christ the Lord, for all people."

"Yes," said another shepherd as the others quit talking, "and the heavenly angel said, 'Peace' to everyone on whom God's favor rests."

Mary had been sitting up quietly in the bed; her arm was stretched out with her hand touching the manger. She heard some of what the shepherds were saying and called to Joseph. "Joseph, their message is similar to what we have both received."

Joseph agreed, looked guardedly at Jesus, then glanced toward the gate door and said to Mary, "I believe their messenger was an angel of the Lord. I believe God sent them." He looked at Jesus, then over to Mary. "Let's bid them to enter," Joseph said, "but we will not allow them to hold him."

Mary nodded, saying, "Yes, Joseph, you may bid them draw near." She knelt by the side of the manger, and Joseph stood near them.

The shepherds came quietly into the stable, and Mary invited them to the manger to see Christ, the Savior born for them, for all people. Some knelt as they came near and placed their hands upon the manger. The oldest one kissed his hand, and after touching his chest, he bowed at the sight of Jesus. The next kissed Jesus' hand and reached to touch the baby's face as he bowed low to look at his Savior. The shepherd wept, and a tear fell upon Jesus' cheek. Jesus opened his eyes at that very moment, and the shepherd dropped to his knees.

After the shepherds had approached Jesus, they spoke with Mary about what they had heard from the angels in the field and what they were witnessing now. "You and Jesus are the sign we were to find." One shared verses from the prophecies that foretold Jesus' birth.

After telling Mary these things, they knelt and began giving thanks and praise to God for the birth of Jesus and pronounced blessings upon the family.

Joseph stood by Mary, who had remained on her knees, and he, too, gave thanks to God for his wife and the birth of Jesus. He praised and thanked God for the confirmation and affirmation of the angelic messages he and Mary had received and prayed blessings upon the shepherds and the message they would be proclaiming.

"Lord God, I praise and thank you for the gift of your son and for Mary and her courage. Thank you for sending the heavenly host to the shepherds to tell them to come find us. Their visitation has confirmed all that you have revealed throughout the ages. Bless them with wisdom as they return to their work. Keep us all safe so we may fulfill the work you have prepared for us to do. Amen." When Joseph finished praying, the shepherds rose to their feet, offered thanks to Joseph and Mary, and left to return to their flocks.

Mary pondered everything she had heard, from the first angel that visited her, to the words Elizabeth had said about her baby and Elizabeth's son. Mary had gone to visit Elizabeth after telling Joseph she was with child. Her cousin Elizabeth, past childbearing age, was also with child, and her baby leapt in her womb when Mary first arrived.

Blessed are you among women, and blessed is the child you will bear! Elizabeth had surprised Mary with this proclamation. Mary had felt a sudden relief as Elizabeth continued, *Blessed is she who has believed that what the Lord has said to her will be accomplished!*

Mary was so happy at Elizabeth's welcome that she sang a new song glorifying the Lord.[2] She told Joseph all about her stay with Elizabeth and Zechariah when she returned to see him three months later.

Mary had been nervous about going to see Joseph when she first returned from her visit with Elizabeth. But she knew in her heart that Joseph would at least listen to her. She went to his shop and walked in confidently. Joseph had no customers and locked the door behind Mary. The scene replayed in her mind's eye.

Mary, I am pleased to see you. I thought you might not return. I wondered...

Mary interrupted him. *Oh Joseph! I am so happy you are glad to see me. I didn't know if you would send me away again or not.*

I'm sorry, Mary. I didn't understand what you were talking about until an angel came to me the night I sent you away. I went to your parents, and they said you had gone to your cousin's house. They didn't know when you would return.

Joseph, I prayed that God would convince you of the truth. When I went to Elizabeth and Zechariah, I learned she was pregnant, and Zechariah had become mute. Their baby leapt in her womb when I arrived. She called me blessed—blessed, Joseph, not cursed! It was such a relief to hear her call me that and affirm God's promise and message. Joseph, she's old, and I worry about her pregnancy, but she is convinced she will be fine because the Lord told Zechariah that he would have a son, and the child should be named John.

Looking at Joseph now, she said to him, "Joseph, John should be about three months old now. Elizabeth was further along than I when I visited. I hope they are all well. I haven't heard anything yet."

Joseph reassured her, "Mary, I'm sure they are all well. God will provide for them just as he will for us."

Mary nodded her head and thanked God for the angels, Joseph, the innkeeper and his wife, and the shepherds. Jesus began stirring and crying softly. Joseph lifted him out of the manger and gave him to Mary so she could nurse him. Then he walked to the door and looked out at the sky. It was early dawn, and a golden glow filled the horizon, announcing the rising of the sun.

"The sun is close to rising, Mary. It has been a short night with little sleep. You must be very tired." He walked back toward her, sat down, rested one arm across his knee, and looked at her.

Mary and Joseph spoke about their visitors while Jesus fed at her breast. Mary looked back at Joseph. "Yes, Joseph, it has been a short night, but it has been very worthwhile and encouraging. I was nervous when the shepherds first arrived, but their witness and testimony was so encouraging. The mystery of God's way is unfolding to us and lighting up the darkness in the world as subtly as the sun rises in the sky and pushes away the darkness."

When Jesus was finished nursing, Mary asked Joseph if he would like to hold him for a while. Joseph smiled and told Mary he would like to take Jesus for a walk in the sunrise. Mary swaddled her son with an extra blanket, bid them to have a good walk, and then nestled down onto her bed to sleep.

Joseph walked around the outside of the stable with Jesus, telling Jesus he was God's son and showing him the world around him. He talked about the people who already acknowledged Jesus and those he would save from sin. As the sun rose up over the horizon, Jesus nodded back to sleep.

After standing with Jesus' head nuzzled into his neck, feeling the breath of God with Us, and marveling at what they had heard from the shepherds, Joseph noticed that the palm of his hand covered the head of the Christ child. Joseph felt weak in the knees as a sense of awe and wonderment overwhelmed him. He looked again toward the glowing sunrise, took in a deep breath, and walked back to the stable where he found Mary, sound asleep in their bed.

Joseph admired her strength of spirit and sense of humility. Her trust in him was growing, as was his confidence in her. The reality of the fulfillment of the prophecy was becoming more and more clear to them. Looking at Jesus, he said quietly, "You are Jesus, the Christ, and God's sign for the whole world. May the good Lord help us to protect you; let no one snatch you out of our hands or his."

After gently kissing Jesus' cheek and carefully placing Jesus in the manger, Joseph laid down quietly next to Mary for a short nap before he would rise and make plans for the rest of the day. They still needed to register for the census, and there wasn't much time. More than likely, they would be packing later today. Tomorrow at the latest, they would be leaving the innkeeper and his wife so Mary, Joseph, and Jesus wouldn't miss the census registration.

When the shepherds who had seen Jesus returned to their fields, they were still rejoicing and praising God. It was early morning, and the sun was rising on the east side of the stream. The animals were already up and moving around; some were drinking from the stream, others grazing in the field. The shepherds who had remained behind to tend to the flocks were preparing a breakfast meal of fish and bread. They began talking about the shepherds who were returning, wondering if they had gotten drunk on wine while in town, and whether or not they had found the sign, the baby wrapped in cloth lying in a manger. One of the returning shepherds called out to them, "Good morning!"

As the returning shepherds began running toward them, the one tending the fire looked up and asked, "Did you find the Christ child?" He wondered if the virgin would have abandoned the baby, and they would be bringing him back.

"Did you find the virgin and her baby?"

"Yes! We did! And his mother and a man with them!"

"A man? Who was he?"

All the shepherds gathered around the breakfast fire. Their conversations were animated as they filled their cups, broke the loaf of bread, and shared it while eating their fish.

"Tell me what happened when you found them."

"We found them in a stable, just on the edge of town. A glowing light seemed to guide us and rested upon the place they were staying."

"Who is the virgin?"

"Her name is Mary, and Joseph the carpenter was with them."

"Joseph! Why would Joseph be with them? "

"You have heard of them, then?"

"A little, perhaps."

"Listen, wasn't Mary the one accused of adultery?"

"Falsely accused, remember? That's why Joseph didn't divorce her."

"Joseph was almost reluctant to let us into the

stable to see Jesus. He was quick to his feet after we looked through the window. He questioned us before he let us in and then only after he consulted Mary and she consented."

"I can imagine we would be the same way. Joseph is guarding them as we do our sheep: no intruders welcome."

"I saw an aura of sorts around them as I drew near. When I bent over to get a good look, Jesus opened his eyes." The shepherd lowered his voice and rubbed his forehead. "It seemed as if he was searching my soul."

"I agree. When I came near and reached out to touch his hand, my knees became weak, and I dropped to the floor."

"Mary barely spoke, except to welcome us. She smiled and nodded as we told her what we remembered from the prophecies that have been handed down to us from our ancestors."

"So, you've seen a child lying in a manger wrapped in cloth, a woman, and a man; and now you claim you have seen the Messiah!" The eldest shepherd doubted all they were saying. "You believe he's the Christ. You could have found another child in another manger in any of those stables with as crowded as the city is!" He pursed his lips and shook his head, looking at the ground. "But did you look any further?"

"No! We didn't have to look any further! We found the child just like the angel told us."

"You found the child just like the angel told you. You foolish men, what have you been drinking to believe these tales?"

"Tales? This is not a tale! This is a prophecy being fulfilled! We are telling you the truth. If you had come with us, you would have believed us."

"Come with you? I awoke with the cock's crow to find you gone. You abandoned your own sheep on your watch. Do you realize what trouble we could have had if they had been attacked? Do you really believe everything you think you hear and see? You ran off in the middle of the night to find a babe wrapped in cloth lying in a manger, and you want me to believe? What? What would the master have said if our flock had been attacked? Did you think even once about that?"

"But the flock wasn't attacked! I prayed for their safety and ours, and God answered!"

"Come! Come with us now! Come with me to see. I will show you. You will see his face and believe!"

"No. No, I am not leaving the flock to chase after some dream you have had. Believe if you want, but don't force me to follow you there."

"Alright, don't come and see. Don't believe for now if you want. Doubt, but a day will come when you will see him. Perhaps then you will believe."

"I've had enough of this arguing. We have work to do. Let us pack our things and get on our way, or our master will wonder about our delay. Is anyone willing to go ahead and see where the rest of our caravan is and if they have set up permanently for the season or not?"

"I'll run on ahead and go over the hill. If I see them set up nearby, I'll go ask if we are to keep the flock here or bring them along."

The eldest shepherd, who had fallen asleep on the other side of the stream, hadn't seen or heard the angel or the heavenly host. The shepherds who had seen them wondered why he hadn't been awakened by the light or the chorus. But they rejoiced in the knowledge that God so loved the world that he gave them his one and only son to save people from sin.

The eldest shepherd always remembered what the other shepherds had told him about what they had heard and saw that night. Secretly, he hoped that one day angels would appear to him with a message of some kind. Each year, the shepherds would remember their experience and re-tell the story. As the years went by, the old shepherd learned more and more about Jesus and became one of his many followers. When the shepherds spoke about Jesus, they referred to him as The Good Shepherd, the one who risks his life for his sheep.

THE FIRST DAY

The First Day

To wake in the morning
With the Christ child in your midst
Not distant or near but here
Tangible and touchable
To hear His cry,
His coo
His sigh
To feel His breath
To wake in the morning
And know His reality
Is not just a dream
To wake in the morning
With God's promise fulfilled
The Savior of the world
Has been born on earth
Blessings of Joy and Peace and Awe!

~June G. Paul~

In the morning hours, everything was still and quiet in the stable. The cock had not yet crowed when Mary woke to the sound of Jesus crying softly, whimpering as newborns often do. She rolled onto her side and stroked his head. Tufts of his dark hair curled around his ears. His fingers curled into a tiny little fist that he tried to suck on. His body quieted at her touch, and he blinked his dark eyes open. His small, perfectly-formed lips pursed together, poised for a childlike kiss.

Mary caressed his arm and with her finger held his tiny hand open: ten perfect fingers; and he had ten toes on such little feet they fit in the palm of her hands. She wondered where they would take him, what paths he would walk, and where he would lead her and Joseph in their lifetime together.

Mary pondered the message the angel had told her: that this child would save people. *How?* she wondered as she turned her gaze toward Joseph and then out towards the late night sky quilted with the golden hues of early dawn in the horizon. Mary whispered, "How, Lord, will you save people through him, through this little child, your son?"

Suddenly the cock's crow broke her chain of thought and startled Joseph awake. Mary looked at him, smiled, and laughed quietly. Stretching his arms up out, he touched Mary's shoulder. She turned back toward him, "Good morning, Joseph."

"Good morning, Mary, did you sleep well?"

"I slept off and on, Joseph, and you?"

"Ahhhh, yes, I'm afraid I may have slept too soundly, Mary. Were you in need of anything?"

"Oh no, Joseph. I was just thinking about Jesus and God's plans for him, for us, for the world." Mary remembered other things the angel had told her about Jesus, but she kept those thoughts to herself right now, for it all sounded a little confusing. She sighed deeply, holding Jesus close to her and looking intently into his face. "How is this baby going to save the world from sin?"

"Mary, such thoughts are too deep for me right now. I cannot understand God's plan to save the world from sin through Jesus. But I do trust the angel's message. I am sorry for not having believed you when you first told me about being with child; it's just... I couldn't..."

Mary placed her finger over Joseph's mouth to silence him. "Shhhhh," she said, shaking her head gently and smiling ever so slightly. "Joseph, it's alright. We are in the presence of God's son. Let's just accept

God's gift of love and grace and give each other the same love. I forgive you, Joseph; I forgave you months ago."

Joseph pushed himself up on his elbow and ran his hand across Jesus' cheek. Then he brushed Mary's hair from her face and kissed her gently on her forehead. Sunlight streamed through the roof beams of the stable like sunlight breaking through a clouded sky. The animals began stirring, and the young couple heard a gentle knocking at the door of the stable.

"Good morning," the innkeeper greeted Mary and Joseph as he slowly pushed the door a little further open. "May I come in?"

"Good morning! Of course, you may come in!" Mary smiled as she welcomed him.

"Come in! Come in!" Joseph called out simultaneously with Mary. "We have a baby with us this morning! Come and see the child!"

The innkeeper smiled broadly and pushed the door fully open. His wife was standing at his side holding a tray. He nodded his head in her direction saying, "My wife has brought a hearty breakfast for the two of you. She said your wife would be hungry by now. I'm certain you are as well, Joseph."

Joseph looked at Mary and raised his eyebrows quizzically. Mary tilted her head, smiled, touched her stomach, and nodded her head at Joseph. Turning back toward the innkeeper, Joseph replied, "Yes! Yes, she is hungry! Of course, we both are." He rose to his feet and walked over to the innkeeper's wife, asking if she needed any help with the large tray.

"No," she replied, "you sit, and we will serve you as we do all our guests."

Joseph walked toward Mary and took the baby Jesus from her arms. As Mary worked herself up to a sitting position, the innkeeper asked if she was comfortable enough. Joseph broke into the conversation before Mary could answer, "I hope you don't mind that I used some of your straw for our bedding last night? I can pay for it or do some work for you. I am a carpenter by trade."

"No! A carpenter, that's a good trade! But no, I'll not take your money. You'll not pay for bedding or food. I would have done the same for my wife. When I told her about your wife's condition, she was expecting you to come and get her for help. It is our honor to have you as our guests. How did you fare through the night?"

"Fine, everything went well!" Joseph and Mary answered in unison.

"The delivery went well then, Mary? And Joseph, you had no trouble? You could have come to wake me. My wife would have been willing to help." The innkeeper's wife drew near and smiled at Mary.

"Where shall I set your tray?" she asked quietly, looking around for a place to set it down.

"I'll bring my tool chest over." The innkeeper grabbed hold of the side and dragged it across the stable floor. His wife set the tray down and stood up. Straightening the apron covering her skirt, she looked down at the baby.

"Thank you so much for thinking of us and treating us so well!" Mary looked up and saw the innkeeper's wife looking at Jesus. "Would you like to hold him?"

"Oh! I would love to, but I'm afraid I wouldn't want to put him down, and I have many guests and rooms to tend to this morning. But if I may come back when my work is done, I would love to visit for a while. Perhaps I could watch the baby while you come to our home and clean yourself up a bit?"

Mary looked at Joseph. "That is a very generous offer, isn't it, Joseph?"

Joseph looked at the innkeeper's wife and smiled gratefully. "It is very generous. An invitation like this would be difficult to refuse. Thank you very much."

"I am honored to be of service to you," the innkeeper's wife answered. "I will return later when my work is done." She and her husband walked together out of the stable and walked quickly back to the inn.

The innkeeper spoke to his wife, "Such a young girl and gentle yet brave couple."

"Yes," she replied, "and they told you they are here to register for the census, correct?"

"That is what he mentioned last night. Will she be strong enough to get to the place and stay in line so long?" the innkeeper wondered. He paused and turned to look back at the stable. "Time will tell. We'll know more later today or tomorrow."

His wife replied, "Perhaps you will have to take them in the wagon." She turned back toward the inn, and they began walking up the stone-hewn steps. She continued talking. "But then, there are other couples with young children, and certainly others who have delivered or will deliver a child on the way."

Back at the stable, Joseph walked to the door and pulled it shut. Walking back toward Mary, he cautioned her about saying too much to the innkeeper and his wife about who Jesus really was. Mary gently nodded in agreement saying, "Some things must be kept in our hearts for a period of time, I suppose."

Joseph agreed. "Perhaps God will send us angels again to tell us when to reveal him to the world."

With that, he picked up the loaf of fresh barley bread the innkeeper's wife brought, gave thanks to God, and shared the bread with Mary. Mary lifted the lid off the nearby kettle and looked inside. The whey was hot and steamy. The sweet smell wafted upward as Mary scooped out a ladle, filled a cup, and served it to Joseph. Then she filled a cup for herself. After taking a sip, she set it down and dipped her bread in the small bowl of olive paste. She set that down and peeled an egg.

"This is like a feast, Joseph! We hardly deserve this. The innkeeper and his wife are certainly very hospitable."

Joseph nodded in agreement as he dipped his piece of bread in the cup of whey and grabbed a handful of grapes. They reclined on the bedding of straw, eating and conversing about the innkeeper and his wife. Mary wondered again about how her cousin Elizabeth was doing and how old their child was. She was concerned about Elizabeth's health due to her old age.

"Yes, and Zechariah certainly has his work cut out for him, raising a boy at his age," Joseph commented. Then he turned the conversation toward Jesus. "We have a responsibility on our hands, too, Mary."

Mary replied, "Yes, Joseph. May it be to us always, and to Jesus, according to the Lord and his will."

"Mary," Joseph held her chin gently and spoke directly at her. "I am going to have to spend more time studying the Torah and be certain that Jesus spends time with the rabbis. But I do not know that it is necessary for us to tell them who Jesus is to us and them."

"Yes, Joseph, whatever you say. In God's time, he will reveal to us what we are to do; we must believe that. It is our shared belief that has brought us safely this far. Now, shall we bathe him? Will you draw some water and heat it, please?"

Joseph got up, and they bathed Jesus together, his first full bath. They laughed at his expressions when they poured the warm water over his head and belly. He didn't seem to like it so much, but he didn't fight or cry, either. They dried him, swaddled him with a clean blanket, and laid him on the covers of their makeshift bed.

Mary lay down and nursed Jesus while Joseph, reclining next to them, leaned against the side of the stall. They all dozed off until Joseph was stirred awake by the muffled sounds of what sounded like a small caravan. He went outside to look.

"Sure enough!" he said out loud, bringing his hand to his head. "They must be coming to register for the census. The census!"

Joseph turned and walked back toward Mary and Jesus. He had forgotten about the census in the excitement of Jesus' birth. He returned to Mary and found her sleeping soundly with the child cradled in her arms. The baby was also sleeping, such a peaceful sight to behold. Scratching the back of his head and heaving a sigh, he turned to look out the window.

Gazing upward, he wondered about the census and the timing of Jesus' birth.

Was it even safe to register Jesus? Joseph wondered. "Why not?" he answered himself out loud. "Who else could possibly know who Jesus really is? Certainly God, who knows everyone and everything, knew the census would be taking place."

"Joseph, who are you talking to?" Mary asked.

Joseph turned and laughed. "Oh, I'm sorry; I didn't mean to wake you. I was just talking to myself. Mary, I forgot we still have to register for the census. I forgot all about it until I heard a small caravan just a little while ago. I don't know how long it will be before you are able to manage."

"I'll be fine, Joseph; we will all do well. Other people have registered with a newborn baby."

Joseph spoke matter-of-factly, "Mary, I think we should stay another night. I don't want you or Jesus to have any problems. You are the good Savior's mother, after all; he is in need of your care. I must take care and protect both of you, Mary." Having said this, Joseph left the stable to find the innkeeper to pay for another night. Along the way, he met the innkeeper's wife.

"Greetings, Joseph, I've got some lunch for you and Mary. My husband is on his way to join us. We thought perhaps we could share this meal together and have a short visit if we may."

"Your offer is very welcome. Mary and I will enjoy your company. She woke just before I left to come and talk with your husband."

The innkeeper walked toward them and joined the

conversation. "How are you, Joseph? It's a good day, eh, when you become a father?"

Joseph smiled and wondered about that. *A father? I'm not a father. This is God's son,* he thought to himself as he and the innkeeper followed his wife toward the stable. His thoughts continued. *People are going to be calling me a father now, and I haven't even taken Mary as my wife yet; we're only betrothed. Well, they don't know that, and I am not going to put Mary at risk.* He spoke out loud, "Yes; it's a good day, a blessed day indeed when one becomes a father!" Joseph smiled while nodding his head and patting his hand on the innkeeper's back.

Once inside the stable, they seated themselves around a makeshift table that Joseph had arranged while Mary was resting earlier. Partially reclining, the innkeeper said a blessing as he broke the loaf of bread then shared it with them. A hearty lamb stew was ladled into bowls by his wife.

"It all smells so good," Joseph commented as he dipped his bread into the bowl.

"She's the best cook around," the innkeeper bragged, "the reason our inn is always full!"

The innkeeper's wife smiled and, blushing slightly, shook her head back and forth; she wasn't comfortable with his compliment. Mary smiled as the innkeeper's wife refuted the compliment. "There are better cooks than me, I know! I've eaten their food!"

Mary answered, 'This tastes as good as it smells! I think your husband just might be right! I haven't even been inside your inn, and I already know I would choose to stay with you whenever we return." The innkeeper looked at Joseph.

"Say, the sky was unusually bright last night for your son's birth. Why, you must have hardly needed that lantern!"

Joseph replied to the innkeeper, "Not so! The lantern was very useful! The sky was quite dark when it all began, or continued, I should say. But after he was delivered, that is when it seemed that every star in the sky lit up."

"Yes," Mary added. "We certainly did need that lantern to find everything, unpack, and get settled. Joseph is correct about the stars. Especially one that broke through the beams in the ceiling; one ray fell upon Jesus' face so I could see him clearly, as if it was broad daylight."

"I noticed the same!" added the innkeeper's wife. "Well, of course, I didn't see his face, but it certainly was a beautiful night sky. The kind I could stay awake all night and watch if I hadn't anything to do in the morning. But you know a woman's work is never done!"

"Nor a man's!" The innkeeper added with a strong, loud laugh, "and I have to get back to mine!" He rose from the table.

Joseph stood up with him. "I wouldn't mind having some work to do this afternoon while Mary rests with the baby. How can I be of service to you? And do you know if you have an empty room for us this evening?"

"Joseph, I am so sorry. I don't have an empty room yet. I'm not sure if anyone else does, either. I haven't spoken to anyone else yet today. Perhaps you want to check around for yourself before helping me with my work."

"Thank you for that advice," Joseph replied. "Is that alright with you if I look around, Mary? Is there anything you need that I can buy while I'm looking for lodging?"

"No, Joseph, I'm not in need of anything yet. We have all we need for now. I'll rest this afternoon and see you when you return. Do you want me to start packing if I'm awake before you get back?"

"No, Mary, don't pack yet. With everyone returning for the census there might not be anywhere else for us to stay."

"You don't have any family here that would take you in?" the innkeeper's wife asked.

Joseph and Mary looked at each other. Mary raised her eyebrows and opened her eyes wide, shaking her head ever so slightly from side to side. "No, no, we don't," Joseph replied. The truth was, he hadn't thought about seeking shelter with relatives because so many were opposed to Mary because of her 'condition.' "None that have a place for us," Joseph said out loud. To himself added, *At least not in their hearts.*

Joseph walked out of the stable with the innkeeper and his wife, closing the gate door shut behind him. Halfway along the path, the three parted ways as Joseph headed toward the center of town. There was one other concern he had with this census. Was anyone still angry enough to stone Mary? He began to wonder about this plan of salvation that God had for the world. If it cost him his betrothed, could it possibly be a good plan? Were they out of their minds thinking that all of this was from God? Were they being deceived? *No, I know we are not being deceived. God has a plan, and he has chosen me to be a part of it.*

As Joseph walked into the city, he heard a familiar voice call out to him. "Hello, Joseph! Good to see you!" An old childhood friend greeted him from a distance, raising his arm in a wave as his voice carried through the street. "I was wondering if I'd run into you during our return for the census. How have you been?"

Joseph greeted him warmly as they drew closer to visit while they walked. Avoiding conversations about his betrothal and the rumors the friend mentioned, Joseph turned the conversation towards his occupation, asking his friend if he was in need of having anything built or repaired.

"No, Joseph," he answered with sincerity. "Not now, but I'll keep you in mind for the future if a need arises! I'd best be getting home before my wife wonders where I've gone to. It was good to see you, Joseph! Stop over if you are able before you leave town." He turned the corner before Joseph could answer.

Joseph walked into an inn. "Have you any rooms for the night?"

The woman answered loudly, "No, no rooms available, sorry!"

The next one looked promising, the door was hinged open, but as Joseph stepped inside, the man at the desk looked up from his register and simply shook his head no. "There isn't a single room open anywhere, Joseph."

"You know who I am?" Joseph asked.

"Of course!" he spoke loudly. "How could I forget you? We were neighbors! I hear you are establishing your own reputation as a carpenter now, Joseph. We could use a good carpenter in this place, perhaps to build another inn."

"Yes," Joseph laughed and smiled, "I am a carpenter, but I won't be staying long enough to build another inn."

"That's a shame, Joseph. We could use a man with your talent and skill here. Are you married, Joseph?"

"I am betrothed," Joseph answered before he could stop himself. Realizing the truth he had just revealed and the danger it held, Joseph raised his right hand over the bottom half of his face, then dropped his head.

"Yes, I heard about this, Joseph," his old neighbor answered. "And I heard there is some disagreement about the two of you. Well, I consider you a good man, Joseph; I think you will do well with her. If you love her and she loves you and you give your life to God, then God will bless you. And if God blesses you, then who am I to take that blessing away from you?"

Joseph raised his head and lowered his hand to his side. The innkeeper looked at him and spoke with compassion. "Raise your head, Joseph, and look at me. Joseph, you have done nothing wrong in the sight of the Lord or me."

He looked at the innkeeper with relief as if a burden had been lifted. "Thank you. Thank you. Yes, we love each other, she is a good woman, and our love is growing day by day. We, too, believe this situation is a blessing from God. It was good to see you! Perhaps we'll be able to stop in before we leave town. If not, we will visit next time we are here. Shalom!"

"Shalom!" The man rose, patted Joseph on the shoulder and walked outside with him. "Shalom,

Joseph! May everything go well with you!"

Joseph returned to the stable, his heart strengthened by the encounter with the old neighbor. He told Mary there were no available rooms. They talked about whether to stay or to move along and camp outside the city. "I do think it would be better to stay here for now, Joseph."

"I agree, Mary; this is good shelter, better than one we could find in the wilderness. I will go and make arrangements with the innkeeper."

Mary bent over the manger they had cleared to use as a crib for Jesus. She picked him up and, cradling him in her arms, took him outside for a walk while Joseph went to the inn. She remembered the joy she had felt when she visited her cousin Elizabeth, the song remained in her heart, and she quietly sang it to Jesus, ". . . My soul glorifies the Lord and my spirit rejoices in God my Savior..."[3]

"Very well, then!" Mary heard the innkeeper speaking loudly to Joseph. "As we told you, you and Mary are invited into our home for dinner. You'd better go now and help her get ready. We will see you soon!"

The innkeeper closed the door behind Joseph and called to his wife, "We have guests for dinner tonight!" They weren't accustomed to inviting their lodgers to dine with them in their own kitchen. However, this couple was pulling on their heartstrings. There was something special about them staying in their stable and the birth of that little boy. If they had a spare bedroom, they would be letting them sleep in their home; but that was not the case, so dinner in their kitchen was all they could provide.

Joseph carried Jesus and helped Mary walk up the rough, stony path towards the innkeeper's house. A cool breeze brushed across their faces as they walked. "How very nice of them to invite us in for dinner," Mary said.

"Yes, it is Mary, and he still refuses to receive any of my money or service in exchange for their hospitality. He said that after dinner, you and his wife will visit while he comes back to the stable and helps me clean it up a bit."

"It will be very pleasant to visit with his wife. The innkeeper is a very good man, and he knows you are one, too. He will be blessed greatly for his hospitality towards us."

The innkeeper's wife had been watching through the window as Mary and Joseph walked up the path. She went to the door and opened it, "Come in! Come in! Such a lovely evening, isn't it? Mary, do come and sit down! You must be exhausted." She pulled a chair from the table and placed a cushion on it. "Sit here, Mary." As Mary was making herself comfortable, Jesus began crying softly.

"Hello, Joseph," the innkeeper said as he walked out of the office into the room. A pipe with a long stem hung from his mouth, and the tobacco smoke curled up and out, filling the room with a pleasantly sweet, warm scent, almost overpowering the smell of fresh bread and the roast on the table. "Sit down! Sit down!"

During the meal, they talked about the shops in town and business. Joseph told them about the man who wanted him to stay and help build another inn. "Why not, Joseph? You said you were looking for work."

"Not that kind of work. Not that large of a task, not now anyway. I have a shop and business to return to and customers who are waiting for items. It wouldn't be right to abandon them just like that. But we can consider our options for the future, right, Mary?"

"Certainly, Joseph, considering options is good," Mary replied and thought, *Is that God's plan? To have us bring Jesus to this place and save the people here from sin?* She had so many questions without answers.

After dinner, the two men went out to clean the stable while the women cleaned up from their meal. Jesus slept during the meal but began stirring now. Mary lifted him up and brought him to the innkeeper's wife. "Would you like to hold him for a while now? I will gladly wash the dishes."

The innkeeper's wife beamed a large smile at Mary. "If you don't mind, that would be so nice! It's been quite some time since I've held a newborn baby in my arms."

Mary smiled and gave Jesus to her. At the basin washing dishes she thought to herself, *You aren't holding just a baby; you are holding the Savior of the world. Oh, it's so hard not to be telling you that. But it's not for me to say. It's news that God will reveal to you and others in his time and way. Perhaps in the same way he revealed this news to me and to Joseph.*

Mary continued washing dishes and listened to the innkeeper's wife singing quietly to Jesus while she cradled him in her arms. Mary smiled. When the song was over, the innkeeper's wife asked, "Have you named him yet?"

Mary replied, "Not formally. We have no certificate

yet, but we will call him Jesus."

"Jesus." The innkeeper's wife said his name again. "Jesus. That has a strong yet gentle sound to it. It's a good name, Mary. You should come and sit down; you've been standing long enough. I'll finish those dishes now." Standing up and walking toward Mary, cradling Jesus in her arms, she asked, "Do you have family members with this name?"

"Why no, no, we don't. But Joseph and I have agreed to call him Jesus."

"He's such a handsome child." The innkeeper's wife was studying his looks as she gave him back to Mary. "Thick hair, good set of lungs, a strong grip, and gentle smile." She looked at them both, then clasped her hands together thoughtfully, "Mary, I've found a few items you might find useful. Some garments and an old carved toy. Could I give them to you? It's a small toy, not much of anything, but I would be honored if you accept it. And the garments I made a long while ago for another young couple, but they did not need them."

Mary hesitated, knowing their bags were already quite full for the journey, but hearing the sincerity of the woman's offer, she couldn't refuse. "It is so kind of you to think of us. We can certainly make use of what you have."

Joseph and the innkeeper were busy cleaning out in the stable. While Joseph was making a fresh bed of straw for the night, the innkeeper asked if they might not prefer to have a separate bed for Jesus. "Well, I cleaned out this manger over here, and we used that this afternoon as a bed for him. I was a little nervous about crushing him if I rolled over in my sleep."

The innkeeper chuckled at the thought and shook his head. "Good thinking to use the manger, Joseph. Let me help you clean it up properly for him." He brought a brush and a basin of water and scrubbed the manger clean, then dried it with a cloth. "Now we can add some bedding in here so it's nice and soft. I brought these clean blankets so you can use them as well. I'll take what you and Mary have already used, and we'll wash them for you."

Joseph gathered up the old blankets and began spreading out the new ones. The innkeeper sat on a bench. Watching Joseph make the bed he asked, "What have you named the child, Joseph?"

"We are calling him Jesus."

"Jesus," repeated the innkeeper. "An interesting name, Joseph. I don't believe I've heard that name before. Do you have family named Jesus?"

"No, we don't." Joseph looked up at the innkeeper and continued speaking. "But Mary and I have agreed to name him Jesus."

"Well then, if you have agreed on his name, it is good. Jesus is his name. Jesus, son of Joseph—it sounds good." The innkeeper placed his hands on his knees and stood up.

As he finished laying a blanket across the bedding in the manger, Joseph thought to himself, *No, it's Jesus, Son of God.*

The innkeeper checked the lantern for oil and wiped off straw dust and pieces from his coat and pants. Then he asked Joseph if they had need for anything else.

"No. Let's go check on the women. Thank you

again for your kindness. How much do I owe you?" Joseph asked again as he stepped over the blanket on the fresh bedding and headed toward the door.

"Nothing, Joseph. You don't owe us anything. I want to ask you something though, if I may."

Joseph hesitated, turned, and replied quietly, "Certainly." Tipping his head toward his shoulder and nodding, he looked squarely at the innkeeper. "You can ask, and I'll give an answer if I know it."

The innkeeper lifted his hat, scratched the top of his head, spit the dust out of his mouth, placed the hat back on his head, and walked over to the workbench. He patted the spot next to him, beckoning Joseph to come and sit by him.

WHO ARE
MARY AND JESUS?

Joseph looked at the gate door and then turned to go sit with the innkeeper on the workbench. The innkeeper breathed in heavily and let it out with a sigh, leading into a brief cough. Joseph waited patiently for the question. He hoped the innkeeper was going to ask him to build something or ask for advice about repairing something. Looking forward to having something to do with his hands and distract him from all that he was wondering about God's plan, Joseph hoped that was what the innkeeper was going to ask him. But it wasn't.

"Joseph," the innkeeper began speaking, then hesitated and looked at the floor of the stable beneath his feet. He took a long breath, held it for a moment, then let it out while he lifted his head and looked back at Joseph. "Joseph, you and Mary are a kind couple. My wife and I are pleased to accommodate you as long as you need, for free. But I am a little concerned for you. You looked as if you had something heavy weighing on your mind when you returned this afternoon." He paused and, taking another deep breath, let out a sigh as he looked up toward Joseph.

Joseph looked back at him quizzically. "I did? I suppose that having a family to care for is weighing on my mind a little. It is much different than being responsible for only me." He patted the innkeeper's knee and began to rise.

The innkeeper pulled him down gently. "Joseph, I had to go into town this afternoon as well and, to be honest with you, I heard some talk that you are being sought after by some people." Joseph recalled the conversation he had with his friend and the old neighbor. Neither had mentioned this fact to him.

"Sought after?" He wrinkled his forehead and rubbed his eyes while shaking his head slightly before looking at the innkeeper closely. "Sought after? What do you mean? What did you hear?"

"Joseph, there are some people spreading rumors that a man named Joseph is coming to the census to register with an adulterous woman." Joseph straightened his back, set his jaw and drew in a deep breath through his nostrils while pursing his lips to keep himself from speaking so he could continue listening. The innkeeper continued quickly. "Now Joseph, we know it's not really our business, but the truth is it may cause some trouble if the Joseph they are speaking about is you. What I mean is, if you are found here, hiding her away, well, I hate to think what could happen to her if she is found, especially found alone. And not only that, Joseph, but some men were also talking about how you had a good carpenter business, but your reputation has been ruined. They said now some people are refusing to conduct business with you and are now taking it elsewhere."

Joseph brushed the innkeeper's hand off his arm. "Yes," he spoke loudly, waving his arm. "I have lost some customers because of their hard hearts and heads." Joseph stood up and spun around on his heel. "But enough! Enough now! I say enough! I've heard enough of this slanderous talk about Mary, about us!" He turned and walked away from the innkeeper. Then quieting his voice he turned back toward him. "Perhaps it's not so much my reputation you're concerned about as much as it is yours. I thought you were a reasonable and kind man."

The innkeeper stopped Joseph before he could say more. "I am! Joseph, I am a reasonable man! My concern is truly for you and your family, not me. If you have something to tell me, please do. I want to help!" He rose to his feet and walked to the small window, looking out toward the fields.

Joseph paced back and forth, and then sat on the workbench staring out the gate door of the stable toward the inn. He breathed in and out to calm himself. The innkeeper walked slowly toward Joseph, speaking calmly.

"Joseph, you can trust me. My wife will want to help as well, if we are able. But Joseph, you must speak the truth to me. Who is she? Who is she, truthfully? Your wife or a scorned woman you are trying to save? And what are you going to do with her and the child Jesus?"

"Who is Mary? You ask me when I have told you already? What kind of question is that? Do you not believe me when I tell you that we are going to register? You would rather believe rumors from people who gossip and slander than the truth from an honest carpenter. We are registering as a family, and we will return home and live our lives simply—as a family."

"Joseph." The innkeeper walked toward him, placing his hand on the top of his shoulder. He spoke gently, "Just tell me yes or no: is there any truth to the rumors about Mary? Is she an adulterous woman? Is Jesus the son of an adulterous woman? This may hinder your lives if it is the truth. People will never accept them, Joseph. Your life will be like that lived by the outcasts."

Those who were cast out of their families did not have easy lives. Joseph was well aware of this. But the command for him to not be afraid of taking Mary as his wife gave him confidence to trust God in this matter. He believed Mary even if no one else did. He also had never been with a woman. He had to risk sharing the truth with this innkeeper. Looking up at the man standing in front of him, Joseph recognized the sincerity of both his actions and his words.

"No," Joseph replied quietly. "Mary is not an adulterous woman. She is my betrothed and . . . well, you asked for the truth, so I am going to have to tell it to you. Whether you believe it or not is of little concern to me, but I am asking you not to question Mary. She has been questioned by her family severely and has been persecuted enough. She has endured much hardship. I will tell you what happened. It is both wonderful and terribly difficult at the same time." Joseph patted the bench and invited the innkeeper to sit. "Come, sit down and listen carefully."

The innkeeper removed his hand from Joseph's shoulder and sat on the stool. Keeping his right foot on the ground, he crossed his left leg over his knee, nearly touching Joseph's. Bending his elbow and resting on his thigh, he leaned toward Joseph, speaking inquisitively. "Tell me Joseph, I'm listening." With a raspy, gruff whisper he continued, "Please tell me from the beginning. I will listen without judgment."

Joseph eyed him carefully and sighed. The innkeeper looked compassionate and sincere. Taking in a deep breath, Joseph turned his body slightly and shifted on the bench. Leaning close to the innkeeper, he cleared his throat and began to tell the story about Mary and Jesus.

"Mary and I became betrothed when her father accepted my request to marry her when she came of age. From the beginning, Mary would come to my shop daily, bringing food or drink so we could become better acquainted. Then, several months ago, Mary came to my shop early one morning. She appeared to be quite distraught, but I wasn't certain because it seemed she might have been smiling, too. I remember well because I had never seen her like this."

"It was early, and the door to my shop was still locked. She knocked hard, for as long as it took me to get to the door. When I opened it, she almost pushed me aside to get in. She was out of breath from running, and tears were flowing from her eyes even as she spoke with, like I said, almost a smile."

"It took some time for her to settle herself down and tell me what had happened. To tell you the truth, I was very angry at first. She told me she was going to be 'with child' and that this would be 'the Lord's doing.' I told her she was out of her mind. I asked her if this was a story she was telling because she had been with a man or because some man had forced himself upon her. She insisted that neither of those things had happened. She told me an angel had visited her in the night. I shook my head in disbelief."

The innkeeper was listening intently. Nodding, he told Joseph to continue. "Go on, I'm listening Joseph, I would be shaking my head in disbelief, too."

" 'An angel?' I exclaimed. 'Mary, you are just a girl. This is unheard of. I have never heard of angels visiting and speaking to girls. You must have had a dream. Are you sure you're not ill? Do you have a high fever, Mary?' I held her arms in my hands, and she was trembling a little. I asked her again if she was ill. Again she said no."

"She tugged at me with both hands pulling away from me. 'Joseph, if I am with child, I could be killed! I could be stoned to death! My family will disinherit me. But Joseph, you, you must believe me! I have not been with anyone. You are fair and just, Joseph. You are a man of deep faith. You must believe me! I am not ill nor am I insane.' She had stopped crying, but her voice was pleading with me to listen. My heart was torn."

The innkeeper nodded his head in agreement. Joseph paused and looked at him more intently, then continued with the story.

"'Your family!' I said to her. 'Of course your family will disinherit you! Mary, I haven't been with you, this we both know! This could bring shame to both our families, Mary. What kind of story is this you bring to me so early in the morning? Where were you last night? Shall I go and ask your parents?' My voice was raised, and she asked me to be quiet, so I lowered it. 'Mary, please tell me you are not with child.'"

The innkeeper nodded again and leaned closer towards Joseph. Joseph stood up and began walking around the stable just as he had walked around his shop that morning. He turned to the innkeeper and continued.

"Mary said to me, 'Joseph, I can only tell you what the angel said to me: that the Holy Spirit was going to overshadow me, and that I would be with child. The angel told me to have courage and be brave. Joseph, can you have courage with me?'"

"What was I to do?" Joseph asked the innkeeper. "I loved her. I wanted to marry her! I had asked her father for her hand, and we were betrothed. I wanted to have a family with her, but with this fuss she was making that morning, how could she dare ask me to have courage with her? The problems this would bring to two families of good reputation."

"I told her no, in no uncertain terms, that if she was proven to be with child, our betrothal would be called off. She begged me not to do that. She kept saying this child was from the Lord, and the Lord had found favor with her. Finally, I had enough. I told her to go away, and I would say nothing. She could leave, no one would know, and it would be a quiet divorce. 'That way,' I assured her, 'you and the Lord's baby might be safe.' I didn't believe her; it was an impossible story to believe."

Joseph stood by the gate door of the stable. He looked out for a while, turned and walked toward the window, then came and walked to the bench where he sat down with the innkeeper. They sat together quietly for a time, neither looking at the other. The innkeeper felt the intensity of Joseph's situation.

Breaking the silence the innkeeper said, "I see," nodding his head and rubbing his beard. "What happened next? She must not have left, or did she? How did you change your mind? How have you endured so much scorn and why, Joseph? You must have a good reason. Some people say you are fair and just, while others say you are a fool."

Joseph crossed his arms across his chest. "People say a lot of things, don't they? I like to think I am fair and just and intelligent. I do have a good reason. I do. But first, I must tell you that Mary did leave. She went to her cousin's house, which turned out to be a very good thing. You, of course, are not going to repeat this to anyone else just now, are you? As I said, Mary has endured much. She is a very strong young woman and truthfully, between you and I, this journey with Mary has strengthened my belief and faith in Yahweh."

"Ahh, yes!" The innkeeper chuckled as he stood up, placing his hands in his pockets and nodding his head. "Yes, women do have a way of causing our faith to get stronger, Joseph. They are not as weak or fragile as many men profess. Your story, Joseph, is safe with me. Your journey is safe with me, too, Joseph. It is your life and your story to share with whomever you are compelled to tell. Thank you for entrusting me with it, Joseph. So go on, I want to know what else has transpired."

Joseph relaxed and uncrossed his arms. He pushed his hands on the bench to straighten and stretch his back some. "So yes, I was angry, and rightly so, I thought. I thought my betrothed was trying to trick me and using the name of Yahweh and his angels in vain. My blood nearly boiled at the thought. I asked, rather, I told her, to leave. The truth is, I myself felt like casting the first stone, right then and there, but I loved her at the same time. I didn't want to hurt her in my anger. I didn't know the truth, so I sent her away. As soon as she left, I locked up my shop and left for her father's house to tell him the betrothal was off, that I wanted a quiet divorce and would settle with him right then and there." Joseph looked down and smiled as he remembered, "I found myself walking toward the synagogue instead."

"The synagogue?" The innkeeper raised his eyebrows. "Aye! I would have gone to a nearby inn for a swig of ale, Joseph! You must be a very righteous man."

"A righteous man?! Oh, not so righteous." Joseph shook his head no and placed his hand on his forehead. "Did you not hear that I wanted to cast the first stone? I think the Lord controlled my steps that morning. God knew it was better I go to the synagogue and pray than go to Mary's father or, as you say, to the inn and get drunk and put the girl I love and the one he set aside for his own purpose in trouble. If I am considered righteous, it is only the Lord's doing in me and not my own."

"Alright, alright, Joseph. But what happened in the synagogue? Did you talk with someone? What happened there?" Joseph looked at the innkeeper and paused as he turned his head away and shook it slightly.

"Nothing! Nothing happened. I left the synagogue as disgruntled and torn as I had gone in. I prayed the prayers but did not sense any effect. I searched the scroll and found no answer." Looking back at the innkeeper, Joseph continued, "I was deaf and blind by my own anger. That is all I could sense. That and dread; I feared for Mary. I went back to the shop and worked on the table I had been making for our wedding day, and I talked out loud late into the evening to myself and to God."

Joseph clasped his hands tightly. "I wanted to understand. I told God I wanted to know if what Mary had said was true. I questioned the Almighty about angels and my betrothed being with child. I told God I did not think I could marry her and that I was going to visit her father and call the betrothal off the next day."

The innkeeper stroked his cheek and bearded chin while nodding his head up and down and back and forth. "I've talked out loud to the Almighty on occasion myself, Joseph." Patting Joseph on the shoulder, the innkeeper continued, "I can't say I ever got a straight answer or heard the voice of an angel in response, but I can say it has calmed my nerves and tamed my anger. So tell me, what happened next?"

Joseph looked away from the innkeeper, tilting his head downward toward the freshly made bed of straw in the manger for Jesus. "Quite simply, I went home and fell asleep. I had a dream. In the dream, an angel of the Lord appeared and told me that Mary was indeed with child, and the child was from the Holy Spirit. The angel told me to have courage, to take Mary as my wife, and to not be afraid of doing so." He glanced toward the innkeeper, who had his gaze fixed on the manger, as well.

"This babe, Jesus, is from the Holy Spirit? Mary hasn't been with any man?" The innkeeper wrinkled his eyebrow, moved his head slowly from side to side, and put his hands on his hips. "Well," the innkeeper breathed in, "I don't believe I've ever heard of such a thing happening. But I've never dreamt of angels, either, nor have any visited me. You say this truthfully then?" He questioned Joseph, staring straight into his eyes.

Joseph looked right back at him, nodding his head and saying, "You asked for the truth, and I've told it to you."

The innkeeper replied, a little dumbfounded, "Then... well..." he sighed while shaking his head again back and forth. "As hard as it is to believe, somehow, I don't know why, Joseph, but I believe you."

Joseph nodded. "Yes, I know it is difficult to believe. The dream was not like any other I've ever had. It seemed so real. I wasn't sure if I was sleeping or awake. The room filled with a presence, a very large presence. This presence was so engulfing it caused me to tremble. Then the angel seemed to draw even nearer to me and said we should call the baby Jesus, because..." Joseph paused, looked at the innkeeper, over toward the manger, and then continued in a whisper, "because he will save people from their sins."

Both men remained silent with their eyes fixed on the empty manger bed. Rising together, they walked and stood in front of it and turned toward each other. Joseph's eyes welled up with tears and his voice quivered, "He's already saved me. How many more will he save? God only knows! I am to have courage in protecting both the Savior and his mother Mary. But with people spreading false rumors about Mary, well, she certainly could be in trouble. I don't want her to know that kind of scorn, or Jesus to know it either."

The innkeeper raised his arm up to Joseph's shoulder and held it there firmly. He looked at Joseph squarely in the eye and said, "Well, God brought you all safely to my inn, and you gladly took this humble stable for the birthing place of a child given by the Holy Spirit. What else can I do? My wife and I will help, but Joseph, may I tell her? She is trustworthy, and she's taken Mary and Jesus into her heart already."

"You may. Since you believe God brought us here, then I have to trust that you two will be a shelter for us all. Our families have rejected both of us; they are ashamed of her condition and do not accept what she has told them. Her cousin Elizabeth did, but she is far away. We could use parental figures, people who will treat us as family about now. We want to share our joy with others, but we must be cautious at the same time. Mary and I have been so appreciative of your hospitality. I can't thank you enough for being able to entrust our news with you."

The two men turned away from the manger and walked out of the stable. After closing the gate, the innkeeper and Joseph walked side by side up the path toward the inn while they talked and laughed along the way. The innkeeper held his tongue while they shared a drink as Mary and his wife finished going through garments and blankets in the in the other room. When the women joined them, Mary spoke first.

"Look, Joseph! A strong basket for carrying Jesus!" She handed it to Joseph, then took Jesus from the arms of the innkeeper's wife and tucked him into the basket. Looking at Jesus, Joseph recalled the story of Moses being hidden away in a papyrus basket. The innkeeper winked at Joseph as the young couple bid them a good evening. He and his wife stood in the doorway on the stoop, watching the young couple walk back to the stable.

"They are so kind and generous towards us, Joseph. I'm growing rather fond of her. She's almost like a mother to me."

"I suppose she is, Mary, and he is like a father to me. Perhaps God brought us here just for that reason." He put his arm around Mary's waist and held her close as they found their way down the steps to the stable.

"Such a nice young couple, aren't they?" the innkeeper's wife said as they turned to walk back inside. The innkeeper was filled with a sense of awe and wondered how he was going to tell his wife that the Messiah was sleeping in their stable, lying in a manger filled with straw. He feared she wouldn't believe him, that she would tell him he was gullible and foolish.

He was compassionate and, sometimes, it's true, a guest or two had taken advantage of him, and she would scold him for that when it happened. Not that she wasn't generous and caring herself; it's just that she had a discerning sense about her that helped balance their business and life together. Because of her ability to discern and her deep sense of caring for this couple, he had confidence in sharing what Joseph had told him.

"Would you like to have another bit of ale while I finish cleaning before we retire for the evening?" the innkeeper's wife asked.

"No, thank you. Why don't you just come over to the table and sit with me a while instead of cleaning? I have something to tell you."

She walked over to the table saying, "Something to tell me? I wondered if something was wrong. You seemed quiet when you and Joseph returned from the stable this evening. Especially after Mary spoke to Joseph. Is something wrong?"

"No, no, nothing is wrong. Rather there is some stirring news that everything is going well and will be quite alright. But you see, when there is a fulfillment of a promise there are perhaps some troubling times and challenges that come along with the fulfillment."

She raised her eyebrows and opened her eyes wide. "The fulfillment of a promise? What promise? Did you promise them something, or has Joseph promised us something? What have you gotten us into this time?"

"Nothing, I haven't gotten us into anything! But something has come to us. No, not something, someone. Woman, are you ready to hear some good news?"

She turned her head and looked at him sideways while questioning him excitedly. "Someone? What? Good news? Yes! Yes, of course, I am always ready to hear good news!" She pulled her shawl over and around her shoulders. "You had me worried. Good news is worth putting the cleaning off for a night."

She sat across the table from her husband. The lantern flame flickered as its light danced around the table. She moved the lantern from between them and reached her hands across the table toward her husband. "Do tell me this good news you have to share! Tell me what promise has been fulfilled."

THE GOOD NEWS

"This might be difficult to explain, harder still to even understand, but I believe it to be the truth," the innkeeper said to his wife as they held hands across the table. "Joseph and Mary, well, they are . . ." As he stumbled over words and looked down, he tried to sort out his thoughts. She waited patiently, releasing her hand and touching his arm. Still looking down, he slowly moved his other hand and bent his elbow so he could rest his jaw in his palm. He chewed on his lower lip while nodding his head slightly before he looked up and leaned toward her. Speaking quietly, almost whispering, he continued.

"Mary and Joseph are very special people to God. Yes, they are not an ordinary couple, not like you and I, and Jesus is no ordinary child." He took his hand off his jaw and patted her hand, then crossed his arms on the table. She did the same and asked him to tell her more.

"I think—now—well, Joseph didn't tell me this, but from what he told me and from what I heard in town during the midday hours, I think, I believe, that Mary and Jesus may be, well, are actually, the sign the prophet Isaiah spoke about in ages past."

"The sign? What sign? Why, I don't even know what Isaiah spoke about signs. Please, what did you hear in town? What did Joseph tell you, and what sign do you believe Mary and Jesus are?"

"Woman, I heard in the streets some people talking about a man named Joseph, a carpenter, who was coming to register for the census with a woman and her child. They said she was an adulterous woman.""

"What? Mary is an adulterous woman and he is hiding her? Well, good for him, I say! And good for her and the child! The men who stone women to death should be ashamed. They don't even obey the commands given to Moses. But this could be troublesome for us—and what kind of sign would Isaiah have been talking about?"

"Well, that is what some of the people are saying about Mary— not Isaiah or Joseph! Just let me finish telling you the story. And don't say anything to anyone. I did not tell them that we had a man named Joseph staying here with a woman who just gave birth. But I did question Joseph this evening."

He lifted her hand in his, pulled it gently toward him, and gently placed a kiss on her fingers. Smiling, he said to her, "I am blessed to have a woman like you for my wife. This will not be troublesome for us. Let me tell you about the sign Isaiah the prophet spoke of."

His wife smiled briefly, then rolled her eyes and asked, "Is this going to be another one of your long stories, or will you keep it short and get to what he said right away instead of keeping me wondering and waiting?"

"I'll keep it short. Now shush; quit asking questions and just listen. Isaiah prophesied to the people who were grumbling with discontent that God would give them a sign. And the sign, he said, would be that a virgin would bear a son and his name would be Immanuel." [4]

His wife interrupted him, "A virgin? Well, Mary and Joseph are married and named their son Jesus."

The innkeeper answered, "Jesus, Immanuel, God with us—Jesus, Yahweh, Jesus saves. They are the same and very similar. But more importantly, Joseph told me more. He told me Mary is not an adulteress, nor has he taken her as a wife yet. When I asked him about the rumors, he became very angry. I told him about what I had heard in town, and he closed my mouth quickly. He said Mary has been through enough persecution, and he won't stand to hear her slandered from us. So I asked him to tell me the truth about them."

Leaning toward her husband, the innkeeper's wife asked, "The truth, yes, and what did he tell you this truth is? How can a virgin give birth?" She sat back and folded her arms, waiting for a reply.

The innkeeper crossed his arms and placed them on the table. Leaning across the table, he answered his wife. "I know it is hard to believe. But he agreed that we should hear it, so let me finish. I told him if they were in some kind of trouble we would help them if we can. That's when he told me what happened to Mary, and I believe him."

"He said she had gone away for a period of time, that he had sent her away so he could think about what she told him before his anger got out of control. During that time, while she was away, he went to the synagogue, then went home. He decided to wait before writing a letter of divorce. He thought he should wait to see if any men would come forward to accuse Mary of adultery. No man ever came forward to accuse Mary of adultery. Despite the rumors, no one accused her. That very night he had a dream."

She shook her head and almost laughed, "A dream!

You take so long to tell me about what is happening. Where did Mary go? Did she go back home?" The innkeeper's wife stood up and walked to the window. "Get on with it! You are squawking like a goose, and I just want to know what happened to Mary and Joseph to make you believe Mary and Jesus are a God-given sign to us. Tell me about that instead of the gossip."

"Alright then! Are you going to stand there staring out the window with your mind closed, or are you coming back to the table to listen?" Her husband was a little impatient with his wife and her response.

"You need me back at the table in order to talk? I'll come back to the table then!" She walked briskly to the table and raised her voice a little. "But I am not sitting down. I can hear just fine standing up! Now tell me, what happened to Mary, and who are these people that they are more special than our other guests?"

The innkeeper put his finger over his mouth. "Keep your voice down. You don't want to wake our guests, do you?"

She rolled her eyes and tossed her head while crossing her arms and in a quieter voice asked again. "What happened to Mary? How can she be both a virgin and yet a mother?"

Answering his wife as calmly and quietly as he could, the innkeeper said, "I told you this would be difficult to understand. While they were betrothed, an angel of the Lord came to Mary in the night. The angel told her she was going to be overcome with the Holy Spirit, and she would become 'with child.' The angel told her not to be afraid. In the morning, she went as fast as she could to Joseph's shop, and when she told

Joseph, he became very angry."

"An angel told her this, and she told Joseph?" The innkeeper's wife raised her arms in disbelief and continued, "I don't know what to think! Angry! I think you would be, too, if I spoke such things to you. You would think I was out of my mind with a fever or something."

Nodding his head in agreement, the innkeeper answered excitedly, "Precisely! That's what Joseph thought, and she insisted she was not ill. He had a difficult time believing the angel part, but she convinced him she was with child. He told me when she kept saying she was with child, he wanted to cast the first stone himself. But at the same time he didn't want to, because Joseph just couldn't bear the thought of condemning and stoning the woman he loved. So he sent her away. He is a good man, self-controlled and righteous. When she left his shop that morning, Joseph closed the shop and spoke to God. He was going to go to Mary's father to tell him the betrothal was off and that he would write a letter of divorce, but he went to the synagogue instead."

"The synagogue? Joseph went to the synagogue? Did he talk to a rabbi then?"

"No! Joseph still hasn't talked with a rabbi; at least, I don't think he has; he hasn't said he has." The innkeeper looked off to the side while he was talking and started rubbing his beard and chin.

She hated it when her husband did that because it meant he was distracted with his own thinking. "Squawk! Squawk! You are sounding like a goose trying not to get caught again. Finish telling me what happened!" She sat down and folded her arms on the table in front of her.

Her husband stood up. She looked at him, smiled and said, "What?! Now you are going to stand up when I just sat down?"

"Woman," he replied, "I can talk standing up as well as you listen standing up! Stop grumbling and listen again so I can finish!"

"I'm listening! I'm listening!" She looked up and smiled at him, raising her forearms and cupping her hands together to hold her chin.

"After Joseph left the synagogue, he went back home. He still thought he was going to divorce Mary, but it was late, so he put off going to her father's house and went home." He walked away from the table and looked out the window. "That night he was visited by an angel, too."

Dropping her hands to the table in disbelief, she asked, "An angel visited Joseph, too? Aye! This is the truth being told? Angels visiting people with such news is good? It sounds like their messages have caused a lot of trouble for them." She rose to her feet and walked over to her husband. Looking out the window with him, she touched his hand and gently asked, "What did this angel tell Joseph?"

Still looking out the window, he replied, "God's angels do not cause trouble. Evil people cause trouble, evil people and evil spirits. Angels from God proclaim God's messages. People listen, believe, and obey; or they dismiss the angels, missing the message and disobeying." He paused; they turned toward each other as he continued, "Mary and Joseph did the first. They are not just ordinary people; both of them listened, believed, and have obeyed."

"Alright." Looking up into his eyes, she nodded her head as if she understood. "But I still don't know what the angel told Joseph. Tell me about that so I can learn how to listen and obey in case God ever sends an angel to me. That's a terrifying thought! I would be shaken to the depths of my soul."

"And they were! The angels told them not to be afraid, so they found encouragement and gained strength from that. Joseph's angel told him not to be afraid to take Mary as his wife, that he shouldn't divorce her." He paused and looked toward the door. "The angel told Joseph that the child Mary was carrying was from the Holy Spirit, and they should marry and name the child Jesus."

The innkeeper's wife interrupted her husband. "The angel told Joseph to name the child Jesus? The angel told him what to name the baby? Why?"

"Because," the innkeeper said emphatically, "he would save people from their sins. And Joseph told me that Jesus has already saved Joseph from his own sin."

Shaking her head in disbelief, she replied, "Joseph said that Jesus already saved him? How can that be? He is just a baby!"

"Yes! Exactly! That's what I thought, too." He was nodding his head in agreement, then looked down and spoke slowly and quietly. "Joseph said he was saved by Jesus as soon as he saw him. He remembered how he hadn't believed Mary, how he had doubted God's message and promise. He remembered how he had wanted to stone Jesus' own mother when she first came to him. It is really only after seeing Jesus that he finally knew for certain that he had done the right thing by not divorcing Mary. If he had, Joseph said, Mary might have been killed, and Jesus would have been killed, also."

"I see, yes, that would have been terrible," the innkeeper's wife said. Then she added, "As a matter of fact, some of the laws don't go along with the commandments given to us through Moses, do they? I've always thought that. Maybe Jesus will save a lot of lives! This is indeed good news! And we should definitely feel honored to be a part of this saving grace. Yes, yes, this is all wonderful news! Now, I have a batch of bread to prepare before we go to sleep."

While she went about her business of mixing the dough, her husband sat at the table to look over their finances. While kneading the dough, all the good news she had heard began to settle into her soul. The Savior, unknown in the world, known in the heavens, came to be born in their stable, to save people from their sins. There was so much to comprehend.

Every now and again, the innkeeper paused from balancing the ledger and glanced at his wife or out the window toward the stable. *This baby was born to bring some stability to the lives of many people by saving them from sin,* he thought. *Lord knows, I've seen enough of it in my lifetime.* There were days when both he and his wife wondered if God was ever going to hear their prayers. This experience was renewing his hope and trust in God's favor toward the world he created. Seeing that his wife was covering the bread, the innkeeper closed the ledger, stood up, and walked toward her.

"We should retire for the evening," he said, stretching. "Morning will come soon enough. Remember, you can't tell anyone just yet. If you do, we could put them all, Mary and Joseph and the baby Jesus, in grave danger, and we don't want to do that! Let us put out the lamps and..."

His wife interrupted him. "This is such good news it will be hard to contain my tongue, but I will, until I have permission to speak. God is doing good things right in our own home, how wonderful! Why, I would never have thought we would be part of God's plan of salvation. This is a humbling position to be in."

The innkeeper put his hand on his wife's shoulder. "I don't believe there is anything in the Scriptures about us, woman. But I do believe Mary and Jesus are the sign Isaiah was prophesying about. I don't know if Mary and Joseph believe it. I don't know if Joseph has even thought about it. He didn't say anything about it."

Speaking with respect, the innkeeper's wife answered calmly, "I believe you. I believe what you are saying is the truth. Now, we can stay awake and stand here all night talking about this, or we can go to our room and fall asleep thinking about it."

The innkeeper nodded his head and laughed, then took her into his arms and held her. Turning, they walked past the window and paused, looking at the stars and toward the stable. "Immanuel, God with us, sleeping in our stable, lying in a manger." He spoke the words quietly. His wife nodded and whispered, "God with us, in our stable, such knowledge is too deep to comprehend and yet, somehow..." her husband's voice joined hers as they both turned toward each other saying, "I believe it's true."

After Mary and Joseph had returned to the barn, they set the basket Jesus was in on their bed of straw. Jesus had fallen asleep on the walk back but began stirring as soon as they set him down. "Look at how small he is, Joseph. It's hard to imagine that this child is actually God with us. I never thought about God being so childlike. So... so helpless... so dependent on us... Joseph, what if..."

Joseph came and stood near Mary. Stooping over, he lifted Jesus out of the basket and brought him to his shoulder. "God with us, Immanuel, Jesus, I love you like you were my own son and yet, you are my Savior." He looked at Mary with tears in his eyes. "Thank you, Mary."

"Thank you? You are thanking me for what, Joseph? I haven't done anything. God has done all this." She sorted through the blankets and asked Joseph which one he thought they should swaddle Jesus with for the night.

"The lighter one, Mary, it's warm enough this evening for the lighter one. And he'll be warm in the manger."-

Mary stared at the manger, "It seems like the manger is so cold and hard, Joseph." She looked back over to Joseph, "I don't mind if he sleeps on our bed."

"Mary, he will be fine in his own bed. We have filled it with plenty of straw, and the blanket is warm. The sides of the manger will keep any breeze away. And I won't have to worry about crushing him while I sleep." He smiled, and she nodded, saying she understood. "If you would like, Mary, I can put another blanket over the straw."

She smiled while looking at Jesus. "I would like that Joseph. His skin is delicate so I think it will be better for him."

Joseph lowered Jesus into Mary's arms. "And as far as you thinking you haven't done anything, Mary, and deserve no thanks from me, you are wrong. You have done so much. You are so courageous and brave, and I am also impressed with your humility, Mary. It makes you that much more attractive to me. I knew you would be a good wife. I just didn't know how good, and I certainly didn't know you would be the mother of the Savior of the world when we became betrothed. Thank you for submitting to the will of God in spite of how challenging it has been and will be."

"Joseph, you make too much of this matter. This is God's desire for us; we are simply his willing servants. I have been his handmaiden, and I feel very blessed to have you with me, Joseph. Any other man would have literally thrown me out and not even listened to what I had to say. Any other man would have stoned me before I went to see Elizabeth and Zechariah. And I don't think they would have had the courage to take me under their roof when I returned."

Mary gently placed Jesus into the manger, turned back toward Joseph, and continued talking. "I wasn't sure what you were going to say when I returned, I only hoped you hadn't spoken to my father. But you are a just and righteous man, called by God to do this work of caring for the Savior. I rejoiced when you told me you had gone to the synagogue to talk with God instead of going to my father."

Joseph put his hands on Mary's shoulders lightly.

"Mary, you are beautiful in heart and mind. How could I turn you away when I love you and when the Lord told me this was all his doing? Truly he has blessed me through you. Any questions I have had about his care for the state of the world are gone now. I know he loves the people of the earth."

"As do I, Joseph. Let us get some sleep before Jesus wakes us."

Joseph closed the gate door and said, "Mary, I do need to tell you something before we go to sleep. You must be aware of how quiet the innkeeper was when we came back to the inn after cleaning the stable this evening."

"I was, Joseph. Is there some trouble? Has he asked us to leave?"

"Oh, no, Mary! He hasn't asked us to leave. In fact, it's the opposite; he said we can stay as long as we want. He even suggested I stay and build another inn." Joseph laughed a hearty laugh.

"That's not a bad idea, Joseph."

"We don't belong here, though, Mary. We are only here for the census. But I had to tell him the truth about who Jesus is, Mary. He had told me there were some people in town talking about us, and he overheard them."

Mary looked surprised and a little worried upon hearing this. "Talking about us? What were they saying, Joseph?"

Regretting what he had just said, Joseph looked away for a moment, then turned back toward Mary. "Mary, don't bother yourself with that. I shouldn't have told you. Ponder the things the angel told you, and don't worry about what people say or think."

"What did the innkeeper say, Joseph, when you told him about Jesus? What did you tell him?"

"I only told him as much as I needed to in order for him to believe me, Mary. I told him about the angel that visited you and how I first reacted. Then I told him about the angel that visited me in my dream, and what the angels told us."

"And what did he think, Joseph? That you and I are strange people in need of help who he wants to see leave his inn?"

"No, Mary, not at all. He believes me. Especially after I told him that Jesus is going to save people from sin and that he had already saved me. When I explained that part, he nodded his head in agreement and said he believed what I was saying is the truth. He said that he and his wife will help us if we are in need of anything. He is a good man, Mary, a godly man."

"Like you are, Joseph. And his wife is also a godly woman, so kind and gentle and loving. Come now, let us sleep, and we can talk more when Jesus wakes us."

Mary and Joseph laid down for the evening. The Prince of Peace had come to earth, and it seemed his peace was filling the stable. Everything was still. There were no sounds in the fields or on the streets. The night sky was clear, and the air cool as a gentle breeze came through the window. Mary and Joseph fell asleep in each other's arms, trusting in the Lord's faithfulness towards them.

DID YOU HEAR
THE GOOD NEWS?

Did you hear the Good News the angels announced?
I heard their cry and their midnight shout
Glory to God in the Highest and Peace to His People on
Earth

Did you hear the good news the angels announced?
I heard their songs clear and strong
I heard their shouts as they crisply called out
Today the Savior was born! (Repeat as echoing and
fade out)

Did you hear the angels cry out and sing?
Did the Good News quicken your heart?
Did you turn from your work?
Did you wake from your sleep?
Did you follow their voices?
Did you look for the star?

Following the star and following their voices
I left everything behind.
Did you? Did you?
Did you go to Bethlehem?
Did you? Did you?
Did you go to see the baby king?
Our Messiah! Jesus!
The Great I Am!
Lying in a manger
So He the Most High
Could live here on earth with you and I!

That's the Good News the angels announced.
Did you hear their songs and their shouts?
Glory to God in the Highest
The Prince of Peace has been born
To save us from our sins (bring peace to our hearts)

Did you hear the Good News the angels announced?
I heard their song and their midnight shout
Glory to God in the highest and Peace to his people on
earth!

~ June G. Paul

You might be wondering:

What must or can I do to have
God's favor rest on me?

Do not be afraid to believe in God.

+

God, I do believe, help me overcome my unbelief!

+

Do not be afraid to believe in the Good News
of the birth of God's Son Jesus.

+

Lord open my ears to hear and my mind
to believe in Jesus.

+

Do not be afraid to receive the Holy Spirit.

+

Lord, I receive your Holy Spirit,
come and remain in me.

QUESTIONS FOR DISCUSSION
Using the Book for Education and Formation

Which character or characters in the story do you relate to?

Do you think you would have offered Mary and Joseph a place to stay?

How do you think you would have responded to the angelic messages given to Mary, Joseph and the Shepherds?

What is sin, and how are we saved from it today?

Do you think Mary and Joseph submitted to God out of love for one another, love for God, or both?

What does this story teach us about faithfulness?

What does this story teach us about betrothal and marriage? How is a betrothal similar to an engagement?

What does this story teach us about adultery and divorce? What did Jesus teach about adultery and divorce?

What is the Good News you should preach?

The following question is recorded in the Gospels of Matthew (19:25), Mark (10:26) and Luke (18:26): "Who then, can be saved?" In each Gospel, the answer given by Jesus is essentially the same: "What is impossible with men is possible with God." What do you think this answer means, and how would you explain it to someone else?

*Go into all the world and
preach the good news to all creation.*

Whoever believes and is baptized will be saved... [5]

ENDNOTES

1   Luke 2:10b-12, 14

2   Luke 1:42 -55

3   Luke 1:46-47

4   Isaiah 7:14

5   Mark 16:15, 16

ABOUT THE AUTHOR

June G. Paul has a B.S. in Psychology from UW-LaCrosse and a M.A. in Religious Studies from Edgewood College. She has served as lay minister and leader in her church, volunteered in schools, founded a parental support group, and provided pastoral care. Her mission is to share the saving grace of Jesus Christ with others through her writings.

She lives with her husband Dale in Portage, WI, and loves spending time with her four children and eight grandchildren.

www.ingramcontent.com/pod-product-compliance
Lightning Source LLC
Chambersburg PA
CBHW060132260626
47160CB00005B/2076